# COMMENTS FROM EARLY READERS

*This book is a treasure for all of us who love animals and is a beautiful gift for all generations! Father Michael's love and compassion for all God's creatures are told through conversations with his sassy cat, Roman Catholic.* ~JUDY SCHIFFER

*What wonderful stories you have written to share. You are a talented and creative writer with a keen ability to relate events with descriptive and interesting details. The stories about R.C. and the other animal interactions offer insight to the bond we share with our pets and the intellect of the animal kingdom. The dialogue form is truly engaging and provides a humorous, yet insightful, Catholic perspective. You have a creative ability and talent to share tales and adventures about R.C. with a writing style that connects with the humorous side of life, religion, and the challenges of different personalities.* ~MICHELE MOORE

*I was finally able to sit and read your beautiful "Stories of an Outstanding Catholic." Father, I loved it! You did a great job! It was heartwarming and your love for Roman Catholic was definit~~~~ ~~~~ ~~~ you to know that it was an abs~~~ you have given me. I will ch~~~* ~DIANE GARRIT~

D1410006

*Father Michael, YOU are incredible! Thank you so much for this treasure! The best gift ever! Having been there for Roman Catholic for so many years, I really loved reading your beautiful journal!*

~JUDY POSTEMSKY

*Fr. Michael, the book you gave us with stories of Roman Catholic was a great, surprising Christmas present! Almost every Sunday when we came to Mass, he met us in the parking lot, checked on the license plate of our car, and told us that our car passed the test! He would not accept tips! He was our devoted parish cat!* ~A PARISHIONER

*Father Michael, the stories of Roman Catholic that you gave me for Christmas were absolutely a delightful reading! Thank you! I am going to share them with others. Have you considered publishing them for the benefit of many children and adults who, too, will greatly enjoy reading them? If you do, you have my support.* ~MARIA ANTHONY

*Love is masterfully woven throughout these remarkable tales! We are given a rare insight into the humorous relationship between a cat and his priest...a relationship bordering on the Divine. The beauty of their extraordinary bond lies in their mutual love and devotion. These captivating stories will be enjoyed by everyone!* ~MARYANNE WATSON

# Stories
# of an
# Outstanding Cat

## Roman Cat✲holic

### (1997-2015)

*Fr. Michael Sequeira*

Fr. Michael Sequeira

WITH ILLUSTRATIONS BY
Dianne Coyle

# TABLE OF CONTENTS

# Acknowledgements

I cannot present these stories of Roman Catholic
to you, the reader, without sincerely thanking some
great people who encouraged me to write them,
guided me, and supported me all the way. Almost
until recently I had never dreamt of the possibility
of this book, but the insight of the following persons
made me begin it and go forward with it. I thank
them and all those who cared for Roman Catholic
through the years. They are:

*Judy and Bob Schiffer* of Clinton, Connecticut.
When I retired from St. Mary's Church of the Visitation in Clinton, Connecticut, Roman Catholic and I
had nowhere to go. Then Judy and Bob welcomed us
to their apartment, which was next to their house at
282 Airline Road. When Roman Catholic entered the
apartment and their house and saw their property,
he had little doubt that he had entered heaven! They
took care of him and spoiled him! His last few years
were an experience of heaven on earth for him!

*Maryanne Watson* of Essex, Connecticut: One of
the most outstanding spiritual, generous, and loving
persons I have ever met in my whole life is Maryanne
Watson. Together with her husband Mark and their
four children, they are inspiring examples of what
it means to practice Jesus' message in the Gospels.
It is the message of love, sharing, and generosity!
Maryanne looked after Roman Catholic anytime we
needed her help. When he rested in peace, she put

flowers at his side and a living plant. It was Maryanne who spent countless hours and days in editing my stories on Roman Catholic!

*Dianne Coyle* of Madison, Connecticut: I can't find words to thank Dianne Coyle for her excellent and creative illustrations for the stories in the book. Dianne's enthusiasm, her creative ideas, and the amount of work she put into the illustrations have inspired me to serve others with that same zeal.

*Judy Postemsky* of Clinton, Connecticut: During the seventeen years Roman Catholic was with me, I needed substantial help in caring for him. It was Judy Postemsky who generously offered that help by taking him to his doctor, giving him his medicine, and caring for him.

*Lena Funk* of Clinton, Connecticut: When Roman Catholic first came to me, Lena was one of the first persons who welcomed him to St. Mary's, took great interest in him and looked after him—especially when I had traveled to learn Spanish and Portguese! She always enjoyed stories of Roman Catholic in my homilies!

*Margo Burke* of Clinton, Connecticut: One of the most devoted members of St. Mary's Church and a great minister to the youth of the parish, Margo always enjoyed the company of Roman Catholic and listening to the stories of his adventures. When I was traveling, she would take him into her home and lovingly care for him!

*The Parishioners of St. Mary's Church of the Visitation* in Clinton: Thank you for considering Roman Catholic as a Parish Cat, for loving him dearly, and for listening to his stories in my homilies. When Roman Catholic was an immigrant (stray cat on our grounds), you supported me in welcoming him to our home and making him an integral part of our parish life.

*Animal Hospital in Old Saybrook:* The doctors and the staff took care of Roman Catholic efficiently and compassionately. Communication between the hospital staff and me was great! Thank you.

*Michael Vogel* of Madison, Connecticut: Thank you for your continuous help and support in getting this work published!

*~Father Michael Sequeira*

# GLOSSARY

ASH WEDNESDAY: Members of the Catholic Church go to church on Wednesday about forty days prior to Easter and receive blessed ashes on their foreheads. This expresses their union with Jesus through self-denial, prayer, and fasting before celebrating His resurrection on Easter Sunday.

BABYLONIAN EXILE: In the year 587 B.C., Jerusalem was invaded by the Babylonians. Most of the inhabitants (the Israelites, who were called the "People of God") were taken into exile in Babylon. This tragedy took place because of their infidelity to God. It was God who had liberated them from their bondage under the Pharaoh in Egypt and had given them a land flowing with milk and honey. They brought sufferings upon themselves by their free choice. Finally, they were set free in 537 B.C.

BALTIMORE CATECHISM: Through the use of questions and answers, these lessons explain the teachings of the Catholic Church.

BAPTISM BY IMMERSION: Baptism is one of the special seven Religious Rituals of the church known as Sacraments of the Church. Baptism is administered by the use of water, normally poured on the forehead of the candidate three times. Historically, the candidate was made to go down into the water in a pool three times, which is called *triple immersion.*

CANONIZATION: The Catholic Church officially recognizes members who practice their faith to a heroic degree by declaring them to be saints. However, the declaration called *canonization* is preceded by a most serious investigation into their practice of faith and their holiness of life.

CUSCO, PERU: In an effort to see and experience real poverty and destitution in some of the countries of the world, I had taken about 200 volunteers from Connecticut and other parts of the United States to Cusco, Peru, to work among the poor between 2007 and 2011. This was a way to make us appreciate our own abundant blessings and to give thanks to God for them. I took them in six different groups for two weeks. We stayed in a modest hotel and helped orphans, children abandoned on the streets, children abused by parents, and children in hospitals. We taught English and built homes for the poor.

EASTER VIGIL: It is a solemn Service on the night before Easter consisting of the blessing of new fire, a special candle symbolizing Jesus' resurrection, readings, baptisms of adults, and the celebration of Holy Communion, which we call the *Mass.*

HOMILY: This is another name for the sermons given during our Services in the church.

LENT: Just as we have holidays and celebrations throughout the year, the Church, too, has special celebrations and seasons. One of them is called *Lent.* Officially it is a forty day period beginning with Ash Wednesday and ending on Easter Sunday. During this time Catholics practice self-denial by abstaining from meat on Ash Wednesday, Good Friday, and on

Fridays of Lent, and by fasting on Ash Wednesday and Good Friday.

MASS: It is another name for the most common form of our Services.

PRODIGAL SON: It is the title of a famous parable Jesus told on the necessity for forgiveness, reconciliation, and peace. You can read it in the Gospel of Luke in the Bible, Chapter 15.

RECTORY: It is the residence of priests attached to parishes. Often it is a combination of church offices and the priests' residence.

ZACCHAEUS: According to the Gospel of Luke in the Bible, Chapter 19, Jesus defied the cultural and religious thinking of the time by staying in the house of a tax collector in Jericho by the name of Zacchaeus. Tax collectors were hated by people and were considered sinners because they were collecting taxes for an oppressive foreign ruler and were extorting people to enrich themselves by collecting more than was due. Jesus was passing through Jericho, an ancient and historical city, and stayed in Zacchaeus' house to show that He had a ministry to all—to the Just and to the Sinners.

# FOREWORD

FOR OVER TWENTY-FIVE YEARS Father Michael Sequeira
was the pastor of St. Mary's Catholic Church in
Clinton, Connecticut. It was the belief of everyone
who knew Father Michael and his black cat, Roman
Catholic, that it was Roman Catholic who rescued
Father and not the other way around. Lena, the
church sacristan, believed that God sent Roman
Catholic to Father to help him retain his perspective
and sense of humor. Roman Catholic and Father's
relationship was one devoted to each other and to
the parishioners of their flock.

Father grew up in a small village in Southern
India. His family grew rice. As a child, Father wit-
nessed how animals were necessary for life there as
beasts of burden, used to cultivate fields, and needed
for food. He saw God's creatures, both wild and do-
mestic, through eyes of gentleness and compassion.

The parish in Clinton was trilingual—hosting
Hispanic, Brazilian, and American communities. To
serve Hispanic parishioners, Father traveled first
to several Central and South American countries to
learn not just the language, but more importantly,
the culture of the countries represented. He then
traveled to Brazil to learn the Portuguese language and
culture. In order that all might have an opportunity to
hear Mass, he celebrated seven Masses on weekends.

When it was time to leave St. Mary's and
retire, Father moved into a home that he had

purchased in a retirement community. He soon found out that Roman Catholic was not welcome in a community where pets were not allowed to wander. There clearly was no question that something would need to change, so Father found a place where Roman Catholic could not only wander about but also expand his ministry.

In retirement Father is as busy as ever. He ministers to the Hispanic community at Blessed Sacrament Church in Hamden, as well as taking Masses in the towns surrounding Clinton. Roman Catholic's spirit is still with us, and Father tells of the life lessons of this precious and God-sent creature.

These stories encompass compassion, love, and hope—precious commodities much needed in our topsy-turvy world. Father and Roman Catholic are blessings in the lives of all those they encounter!

# Make Us a Channel of Love For All Animals

"Then God said, 'Let the earth bring forth all kinds of living creatures.' And so it happened...(and) God saw how good it was." (Genesis 1:24-25)

*Loving God,*

*Creator of the Universe and Giver of all life,*

*we praise You for the beauty of Your creation*

*and the glory of Your Majesty!*

*You created the human family*

*as the crown of Your creative hand.*

*For our well-being and happiness,*

*You endowed us with the precious gift*

*of all animals, wild and tame.*

*Their life comes from You,*

*and at due time they rest in You.*

*May they experience here on earth*

*the justice, respect, compassion, and love*

*with which You created them.*

*May their prayer, "Give us our daily bread,"*
*be answered generously!*
*In life and death,*
*may they receive the compassion and love*
*which Your Son has made known to us.*

*May any oppression and cruelty to them vanish,*
*and may Your goodness be revealed to them!*
*Make us a channel of love for all animals.*

AMEN.

# Just for One Night Please!

In August of 1999, I began to notice a young cat in our parking lot. As I was going from my office to the church daily, he always came to me looking for some food. I gave him none because I did not want to feed somebody else's cat. In an effort to get something from me still, he used to demonstrate to me his skills for climbing trees and descending! Of course, the show was to get tips, but he got none for the reasons already mentioned.

On December 3rd of the same year, somebody told me that he was a stray cat. My heart was moved!

Running to the food pantry in the church, I brought out a tuna can and gave it to him. He ate and cleaned the plate! The next day he was on our grounds again. I clapped. He recognized me, came running to me, and cleaned the plate! On the third day, the same ritual took place except that there was a dialogue.

"Sir, where do you live?" asked the cat.

"There," I told him.

"May I walk you to your house please?" As we reached the door of the rectory, he said, "Sir, please allow me to stay in your house just for one night. I am homeless, hungry, and cold."

I said, "yes, but for one night only. Tomorrow morning after breakfast you are going to pack all your belongings in your suitcase and leave."

He said, "agreed!!!" We shook hands. That night he slept downstairs and I slept upstairs.

When I was fast asleep in the middle of the night, I felt that my right cheek was getting wet. I blamed it on the weather and tried to sleep. But no! My cheek was getting wet! I reasoned that the previous week when I had gone to my doctor for my physical, I had hidden a few things from him and that they were surfacing now! What shall I do? How can I confess it to him? I tried to sleep. But no! The face was still getting wet! I touched it. Something that felt like a snake fell into my hands!!!! Panicked, I put on the lights! Guess what I saw? The cat was sitting on my pillow and licking my face!!!!!!!!!!!!!!!!!!!!!! It was his paw that fell into my hands!

"What are you doing????" I exclaimed.

"Oh, this is my way of thanking you for accepting me. Believe me, you will never regret it."

"What! I regret it already."

"Sir, you preach compassion. Please practice what you preach."

"What! You are preaching to me?" I said in disbelief.

"Oh sorry! Please accept me!" he begged.

"Alright! I accept you but on one condition: that you agree to be a Catholic."

"I agree, of course!"

"Your name will be 'Roman Catholic.' "

"I love it. But when are you going to baptize me? The godparents I have in mind don't go to church, so they may not be eligible. What shall I do?"

"Don't worry! You don't need baptism. By the very fact that you entered the house of a priest, you are automatically baptized and confirmed. Congratulations!" We shook hands!

# WHERE WERE YOU BEFORE COMING TO ME?

ROMAN CATHOLIC WAS HIDING SOMETHING from me! He did not want me to know where he was before he started wandering on our church grounds!

My research gave me some hint. He belonged to one of the businesses which served our needs such as carpet cleaners, flower shops, food deliveries, and altar supplies. He came with them for a ride. When they were delivering the goods, they left the doors of the vehicle wide open.

Roman Catholic jumped out and went for a walk. When he returned, the vehicle was gone! Thus the grounds of St. Mary's became his new home! It was then that he hit the gold mine! He was two years old!

My assistant Lena said that it was God who sent him to me to prevent me from going totally crazy and being admitted to a mental hospital. After all, I was managing all alone in a trilingual parish with a total of 1400 registered American, Hispanic, and Brazilian families. I celebrated seven Masses every weekend in three different languages: English, Spanish, and Portuguese.

# I Don't Need a Doctor!

"Roman Catholic, it is three days since you have been with me. You need to go to a doctor."

"No, I don't need a doctor. I am fine!" he insisted.

"It is the law that you go to the doctor for a checkup and get your shots. Your taxi is ready for you."

Throughout the ride to the doc, he shouted and yelled at me. It was all my fault!

Doctor: "Hi Roman Catholic! How are you?"

Roman Catholic: "I am fine, so I don't need you. Discharge me now!"

Doctor: "Let me see your teeth, Roman Catholic. Friend, you were born in January of 1997."

Roman Catholic: "How do you know that?"

Doctor: "Looking at your teeth, I found out that you were born then. Now, let me give you your shot."

Roman Catholic: "No, I don't need it. Leave me alone!"

During the shot, there was yelling and shouting! On the way home, Roman Catholic said indignantly, "never take me back to that doctor. I don't need him!"

# Today Could be My Birthday!

THERE WAS ONE GOOD THING that came out of the visit to the doctor. Roman Catholic came to know his birthday!

Since then, every day in January and every year upon getting up in the morning, he would say to me, "today could be my birthday! What are you going to give me?" This happened every day, even after it was formally celebrated!

# Call Me by My Full Name

THE FOLLOWING IS A DIALOGUE between a church member and Roman Catholic:

"Hi R.C.! How are you?"

"Don't call me R.C.! Call me by my full name: Roman Catholic."

"How do you like our church, Roman Catholic?"

I have already become an outstanding member of the church."

"How come, then, I have never seen you inside the church?"

"When I said that I am an outstanding member of the church, what I meant was that I am a member standing outside the church building!"

# I Had to Rush Him to the Hospital!

ONE DAY I NOTICED THAT he was very lethargic, sleeping in his corner, and never eating or getting up. I rushed him to the doctor. He had a serious abscess! The doc told me that if I had brought him an hour later, it would have been too late! He had fought with an animal.

He underwent a long surgery, followed by three days of hospitalization, lots of medication, and indoor confinement for a week.

When he was discharged, our challenge began. My friend Judy Postemsky and I tried giving him his medication—which he immediately spat out on the

floor. As for keeping him indoors, he was opposed, so he went on strike. I yielded to his demand and took him out on a leash!

"Oh no!" responded Roman Catholic.

Within no time, he managed to get out of the leash and off he went! He rolled up and down in the dust and passed through bushes with thorns and needles! However, he did recover, and the fur, which had been shaved for surgery, grew back rapidly.

# He Survived Lena's Ire

ONE OF MY MOST DEDICATED AND hard working volunteers at St. Mary's was Lena. Among her many services, growing flowers around the church was one of them. She did an excellent job with it!

One day I received a call: "Fr. Michael, it is Lena. Come to the church right now!" I went and encountered Lena. "See what your cat did," she exclaimed. I saw the area where she grew the flowers. All the bulbs, plants, and seeds were up on top of the soil! Using his strong paws, Roman Catholic had dug it up the night before! Everything was upside down! Lena was angry!

What shall I do now? Should I excommunicate him? Should I send him back to his original place?

"Roman Catholic, come, I want to see you right now!" I demanded. He reported to me.

"Why did you do this?" I wanted to know.

"Oh, Lena planted the flower bulbs four days ago. I did not see any flowers as yet, so I decided to dig up the place and find out what was happening. Her plants, bulbs, and seeds are no good. In fact, they are all dead! They need to be replaced with new ones! It is all the fault of the plants."

"Roman Catholic, please consult with me before you do anything like this again!"

"Oh, you are siding with Lena! It is all your fault!"

# Father, That Was the Best Part of the Whole Mass!

ONE SUMMER DAY I WAS in the church celebrating the Mass. I had left the doors of the church wide open for the air to circulate. Roman Catholic was in the parking lot maintaining order and discipline!

When he heard my voice, he left the parking lot, entered the church, came straight to the altar, and began to listen to me. People were distracted! They were laughing, whispering, and talking.

So I apologized.

Guess what they said? "Father, please don't apologize! That was the best part of the whole Mass! Tell him to do it again!"

# Don't Forget Who I Am! I Am the Director of Ministry to Pets!

Roman Catholic ordered my part-time secretary to put the following announcement in the bulletin:

*Don't Forget Who I Am!*

*I Am the Director of Ministry to Pets!*

*On the occasion of the Feast of St. Francis of Assisi on October 4th, I have organized the blessing of all pets: cats, dogs, elephants, horses, asses, donkeys, fish, snakes, butterflies, and rabbits. The ceremony will start punctually at 1:00 p.m. I will be there to welcome you and your pets and to direct you to your places.*

*Every pet should be leashed except fish, snakes, and butterflies. Once the ceremony begins, there should be perfect silence! Offenders will be disciplined and, if needed, expelled from the location.*

*My Dad will begin with prayers, readings, and intercessions. Then he will go to each pet. He will ask, "What is your name?" Your pet will tell him his name. Then he will make the sign of the cross on each forehead. During the blessing, your loved ones are not to bite his fingers or hand! If they do that, they will be excommunicated right away! Then he will sprinkle Holy Water on them. Reverently, they are to make the sign of the cross and say, "Amen."*

*There is no need to tip me. Just be grateful to me for all that I do for you and for our parish! And if your pets want to become Catholics, please contact me at romancatholic@stmarys.org. I will admit them to our religious formation program and have them baptized at the Easter Vigil by triple immersion!*

*It is Roman Catholic who speaks.*

# Christmas of 2000

THE YOUTH GROUP USED TO donate a Christmas tree to me. One night Roman Catholic came into the house at about nine o'clock. He seemed to be puzzled. I asked him what was troubling him. He said that suddenly a tree was growing in our living room and that we were living in an unsafe building. The foundation could have been cracked and a tree was growing! He went around to inspect it. He attempted to climb it several times.

I explained to him that it was a Christmas tree and that it was a tradition in our country and many other places! It is a beautiful cultural and religious practice!

"I see something special on top of your tree," he said. "You are hiding something from me! I am going to find out for myself your secret!" He attempted to climb the tree several times! It was dangerous, so I disconnected the lights of the tree. I lit the tree only when he was out!

He started drinking water from the basin of the tree! At this, I stopped the Christmas tree in the rectory altogether!

A friend of Roman Catholic's named Kim gave him a Scratching Board for a Christmas present. He loved it! With his teeth and paws, he massacred it! He bit it, chewed it, and reduced it to nothing! She gave one to him for another three years. However, as he advanced in years, he was not really interested in anything. I gave him many Christmas presents, but he would not even look at them. At Christmas of 2015, he sent me an email from heaven, "God gives me better Christmas presents than you ever did!"

I love you, Roman Catholic!

# Your Social Security Number Please!

ONE SUMMER DAY ROMAN CATHOLIC was lying on the grass in a cool place. He was so happy that he thought he was in heaven! Suddenly he saw a cat entering his territory! Right away he got up and went to "welcome" the cat!

"Your name please! Your social security number, please! Do you have insurance? Your cell phone number, please! Why do you enter my territory? How long will you be in the area? What will you be doing here?"

"Roman Catholic, I am not a threat to you! I

only want to take a walk on your church grounds, since they are holy grounds!"

"Oh no! You could be a terrorist! I am the security guard for the church! And I say to you:

Entrance denied!"

"Roman Catholic, why are you so un-Christian? Be a good Catholic!"

"You are never welcome here! If you ever return, I will visit you in prison!"

# Three Strikes and You're Out!!!

Roman Catholic was essentially an outdoor cat, so at 5:30 every morning he would come to my bedroom and begin to sing for me. The message: "get up, open the door, and let me out." I, however, would not grant his request. Instead, I continued to sleep. "Foul ball!" was Roman Catholic's response.

He took a short time off to plan new tricks to capture my attention. Three minutes later he came in. He jumped onto my bed, crossed over my chest, and jumped down to the other side with a big noise. The message: "get up, open the door, and let me out." I did not yield; I just ignored the spectacle. Roman Catholic decided "That's a strike!"

Three minutes later he came in for a third time and repeated his trick. He jumped up from one side of the bed, walked across my chest, and jumped down the other side with a bigger noise! The message: "get up and let me out now!" My response was to yawn and continue to sleep. "Strike two!" was his response as he left again.

Three minutes later he came in for the fourth time and repeated the earlier scenes. He jumped up again, walked across my chest, and jumped down to the other side with the loudest noise yet! The reason: he wanted me to let him out now! However, I continued to be sleepy!

Three minutes later he came in, and guess what he said? "Three strikes and you're OUT!" To put me out, he jumped onto the little table I had with bedtime reading material and began to tear the papers with a loud, crunchy noise! At that time, I got up, opened the door, and let him out. Once outside the door, he turned around and said to me, "I won! You lost!"

Every night when I was at my computer desk, he would jump onto it and block the monitor by sitting directly in front of it. He would say to me, "Tell me, how many boring homilies did you give today?"

And I would say to him, "Tell me, how many cats did you fight with today and did not win a single fight?" He would be quiet because he did fight and did not win a single one!

# Faced Deportation?

ROMAN CATHOLIC CAUSED A MAJOR change in my life. When the time for my retirement came, I was hoping to retire to India where I was born. Therefore, I had retained my Indian passport all these years. The new development forced me to change my plans. How can I leave him behind and simply go away without him? He would have cried and asked, "Why did my Dad abandon me? What wrong did I do?" I could not have left him and gone!!! I would not have been able to eat, sleep, and be healthy! After all, we were going to be together for life!!!

So I applied for American citizenship. While interviewing me on my eligibility, the official in the Immigration Office in Hartford said to me, "Please raise your right hand and promise to tell me the whole truth and nothing but the truth."

I said, "I do."

The official continued: "I will ask you some questions. While answering them, remember that you are under oath!

"1. What is the White House and who lives there?"

I was tempted to put some humor into my response and say, "The White House is my house, and Roman Catholic and I live there!" I felt like saying that because my rectory was a small white building.

Everybody used to point to that building and say, "That white house is Fr. Michael's house. Roman Catholic and he live there." However, I realized that I had taken an oath to tell the truth. There was no room for jokes. So I gave the right answer: "The President and the First Lady live there."

There was another reason for me not joking with the official. If I had said that Roman Catholic lived there with me, the official could have inquired, "Who is Roman Catholic and what is his social security number?" The Immigration Office could have investigated into his background, and found out that Roman Catholic was a stray cat and not documented! In this way he would have been considered an

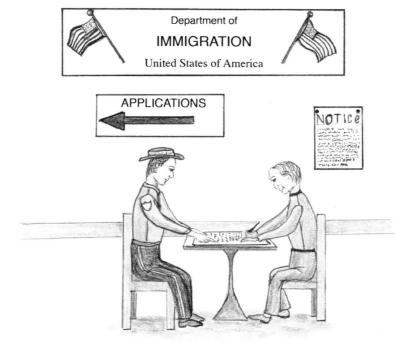

illegal immigrant. Roman Catholic would have been deported!!! I was glad that I had never mentioned the name of Roman Catholic.

"2. Where is the White House?"

I could have joked again by saying, "Oh, it is in Clinton, Connecticut, because the white building, my rectory, is in Clinton." However, I had taken an oath to tell the truth, so I gave the right answer.

The official declared that I had passed the test! Roman Catholic and I were going to live together for life—for better and for worse!

# WHAT ARE YOU COOKING AND WHERE IS MY SHARE?

EVERY NIGHT WHEN I WAS in the kitchen preparing my dinner, he would come to me, no matter where in the house he was, and say, "What are you cooking and where is my share?" He would harass me until I gave him his portion.

Most of the time I had foreseen the situation and was prepared. I had a good piece of chicken breast cooked rare. He would eat the whole piece and then stare at me: "May I have seconds please?"

I would give him another piece. Then he would bite me! That was his way of thanking me! Occasionally, I was not prepared for this scene, so I had to take out of the freezer a piece of chicken, quickly thaw it, cook it in the microwave, and give it to him. He would impatiently ask, "How could you have forgotten me?"

Every night before going to bed, I had to leave his midnight snack on his plate. Upon waking up, I noticed that he had eaten everything and had cleaned the plate.

However, once a year on the night prior to his doctor's visit, I did not do that. He had to fast! Oh, he would jump onto my bed and stare at me! You should have seen his eyes, his tail, and his body language all saying "How dare you not leave me my midnight snack!" It was so true that I was almost tempted to get up and give it to him!

On Sundays after the 9:00 a.m. Mass, I would go to the rectory for a little rest before the next Mass. I would call him, "Come, Meow," and he would come running to me. After reaching me, I fed him. He would say, "Why did you take such a long time to open that can? Couldn't you open it more quickly?"

I said, "You were hungry, Meow!"

He would respond, "Yes, I was very hungry. Why didn't you tell me that earlier? It's all your fault."

# Guess What He Gave Me for My Birthday!!!

THE FIRST THING I ENCOUNTERED upon waking up on my birthday was a present with a note attached to it: "Happy birthday, Dad! This present is only for you! Nobody will ever get such a precious present like this one. Enjoy it!!! Happy Birthday!!!!"

Guess what the precious present was? A Dead Mouse!!!!!!!!!!!!!!!!!!!!

# Roman Catholic on a Diet

At a given time his doctor put him on a diet. When I gave him his diet food, he smelled it, looked at me, and said, "Is this how you save money? You save money at my expense? Where is the garbage basket, please? My food belongs there!" There was yelling and screaming!

I consulted Judy and Bob (the owners of my apartment) because by now Roman Catholic had become a close friend of theirs as well. They often fed Roman Catholic, so together we reflected upon the whole situation. We decided to make him happy during his remaining time on earth! We started to feed him with the best food!

He said to me, "I won! You lost!"

# No Meat on Ash Wednesday and Fridays of Lent

THE ANNUAL CELEBRATION OF EASTER is preceded by a period of forty days called "Lent." It is a time of preparation for Easter. Jesus rose from the dead and entered into a new life. So His followers use Lent to reflect upon their own lives, renounce any hurtful things in their lives, and enter into a new life with Him. The Lenten preparation usually consists of prayer, abstinence from meat on Fridays, fasting, and so on.

> *Ash Wednesday: What?????*
> *No Meat?!?!*

"Roman Catholic, tomorrow is Ash Wednesday. You need to go to church and put on ashes," I instructed.

"No, I don't want ashes. I am black and your ashes are black. Nobody will be able to see them on me."

"It is not something to be seen. Ashes are a sign that you are willing to acknowledge your sins and are going to reform your life. You also have to fast on Fridays of Lent!"

"I have no sins! Only monks fast, not I," he insisted.

"Roman Catholic, the church does not want Catholics to eat meat on Fridays of Lent. You will be eating fish and eggs on those days."

"What? I don't think it is the rule of the church. It is your rule to save money at my expense! I don't eat fish or eggs."

I did not give him meat on Fridays of Lent, so suddenly in the middle of the night, he would jump on my bed and stand on my chest. "What is the matter?" I asked him.

"Do you know what time it is now?"

"No, why?"

"It is one minute after midnight, which means it is not Friday anymore. It is Saturday, so I can eat meat. Get up, take me to the kitchen, and give me something to eat." Reluctantly I would take him there and feed him.

Alas, Easter Sunday had arrived. "Roman Catholic, for your Easter dinner, I give you a choice: turkey breast, Virginia ham, or roast beef. Of these three, which one do you want for your Easter dinner?"

Guess what he said? "GIVE ME ALL THREE OF THEM! After all, I have not eaten meat for the forty days of your famous Lent."

But at Easter... ham, turkey AND
beef rib roast!!!

# It Is All Your Fault!

ROMAN CATHOLIC WAS ESSENTIALLY AN outdoor cat.
During the winter, he would go out, get caught in
the snow, manage to pull himself out of it, and come
home. Upon returning home, the first thing he did
was to bite me! The snow was all my fault, and I
needed to be punished. I could have prayed to God
to stop the snow, and God would have listened to
me, but I was too lazy to pray! It was all my fault! He
would bite me seven times a day!

In the extreme heat of the summer, he would
come home and bite me. The heat was all my fault,

and I needed to be punished. I could have asked God to lower the heat, and God would have heard my prayer, but I was too lazy to pray. It was all my fault! He would bite me seven times a day.

When the weather was really good, he would still bite me! Why? Because the weather was so good that people did not have anything to complain about! There was nothing to talk about! I could have prayed to God to make it slightly different, but I was too lazy to do that. As a result, everything became boring! It was all my fault. I needed to be punished.

# ARE YOU A CAT OR A DOG?

ONE DAY WHEN I WAS in my office, one of the staff members buzzed me: "Father, please come to my office right now!" I realized that there was a big problem.

When I entered her room, she showed me the floor of her office. She had bought a bag of dry food for her dog and had placed it on top of a tall filing cabinet. When she was out of her office, Roman Catholic entered the office, climbed the filing cabinet, knocked down the bag, ripped it open, ate as much as he wanted, and spilled the rest of the food all over her floor!!! She was upset!

"Roman Catholic, come to my office right now," I demanded. "I want to see you!" He came in. I said, "Please be seated." I closed the doors. "Tell me, are you a cat or a dog?"

"I am offended by your question!"

"What you did was bad! You ate the dog food and spilled it on the floor!"

"Oh, I was only testing to see whether the food she bought was good for her dog or not!"

"Roman Catholic," I ordered, "stop giving me excuses! You need to go to confession." He did go to confession, but I cannot tell you what he confessed. I can tell you one thing though: his behavior improved a lot after that!

# A Thief in the Rectory

One night I was fast asleep. Suddenly, I heard some noise in the kitchen on the ground floor. It was the noise of plastic shopping bags and dinner plates. Someone was in the kitchen, was dragging the bags on the floor, and was loading them with my dinner plates. Somebody was stealing my things, but I had secured the doors before I had retired. How could he get in? I was concerned! "I was dreaming," I said to myself and pretended to sleep.

The noise continued to grow! What was I to do? If I went downstairs, my life would be in danger. I continued to pretend that I was dreaming. The persistent noise, however, became a concern.

A few minutes later, the door of my bedroom suddenly opened, and I heard the noise of the plastic bags in my bedroom! The door could not have been locked. The thief had entered my room! He was going to stuff his bags with my clothes. I realized the risk. I covered myself with blankets. As the noise became intense, I put on the light. Guess what I saw? Roman Catholic was wrapped in plastic shopping bags.

I had left some plastic shopping bags on the floor in the kitchen. I never knew that cats get into them and sleep. Roman Catholic got into one of them, but when he tried to come out of it, he got entangled.

To liberate himself, he entered another bag and got himself more and more entangled. He could not set himself free! Luckily he knew the solution. He came to me. I got up and liberated him from his bondage. Guess how he thanked me? He bit me! It was all my fault! I should not have left those bags on the floor! He punished me.

# Prodigal Son

At a given time, Roman Catholic was missing for three days! I looked for him everywhere but without success! People told me that he would come back, but I was skeptical.

On the third day when I opened the door of the rectory, guess what I saw? Roman Catholic was standing there!

I told him that I was disappointed with him.

Guess what he said? "Did you slaughter the fattened calf? Where is the music, dinner, and dancing?"

"What do you mean?" I asked.

"Oh, your Bible says that when the prodigal son returned, the father gave him a big party, so that he and his girlfriend could dine and dance. I went away deliberately in order to get that feast from you with all my girl followers, and yet you have not done anything for me! It is all your fault!" He bit me three times to punish me!

# WHAT ARE YOU DOING IN THE MIDDLE OF THE NIGHT???

I LOVE FISH—NOT ANY fish, but the whole fish with the bones and the head. I clean it and cook it with the bones! It is tastier that way!

One night I was sitting outside on the church grounds and was cleaning a big bluefish somebody had given to me. I had the machete in my hands

to cut its head, tail, and moustache. Suddenly, St. Mary's security guard came rushing to me and said, "Who are you beheading? Is it a parishioner of yours? Is it because you don't like him? What crimes did he commit? I may have to call the Clinton Police."

"Roman Catholic, I am cleaning this fish!"

"What? You eat fish! You cook fish with the bones? Do you have insurance for this? How boring! I hate fish. Give me roast beef always."

# Trick or Treat

One Halloween night he went out Trick or Treating! Guess who he was? He was the Pope! He wore his miter and the scepter. Guess what he did?

"I canonized some cats who were outstanding in everything! I admired their way of life, so I canonized them. They are saints now! I saw some who were so good but not fully perfect, so I praised them and advised them to grow in their holiness. There were others who were nominally good, but there was nothing about their goodness. I ordered them to behave well or else! However, there were some who were really bad! They would not listen to my preaching! I excommunicated them."

When he came home he was tired, and it was all my fault! He said that I wanted him to go out Trick or Treating and he obeyed me! It was a bad assignment I had given him. It was all my fault. He bit me several times to punish me.

# My Sheep Hear My Voice

ST. JOHN'S GOSPEL SPEAKS ABOUT the Good Shepherd in Chapter Ten. In it Jesus says that His sheep hear His voice and follow Him.

I was away for a week. When I returned, I was told that Roman Catholic was missing also for a week. I searched for him everywhere but without success.

I had some idea where he was. Pratt Street, next to the church, has a lot of shrubs and trees. They provide air conditioning to animals in the summer. Guessing he might have been there, I went there at ten o'clock at night and said loudly, "Meow, I am here! Come here!" Within seconds, he was at my feet! Sound travels at night, so he heard my voice, recognized it, and came to me!

"Follow me," he said. He went first and I followed him. We crossed Grove Street, and as we entered the church grounds, he told me that our church was on our left, that my office was directly in front of us, and that we were going to the rectory now. When we reached home, I fed him and he wanted seconds. Then he bit me, which was his way of thanking me.

# Babylonian Exile

Between 2007 and 2012 I had taken about two hundred people in six groups to Cusco, Peru, to work among the poor. We went for two weeks and worked as volunteers with children abandoned on the streets, children abused by parents, children in hospitals and schools, etc.

When I returned, I discovered that as soon as I had left, Roman Catholic had also left. He found a place on Pratt Street and stayed there for about two months. It was a good place for the summertime.

I went to him three times a day and pleaded with him to come home, but he would not come. Given that, I went to him daily and fed him where he was.

He had found a hole in the foundation of one of the homes there, so he had a place to sleep. After Labor Day, however, he came home! Just as the Israelites in the Old Testament went into exile in Babylon, so also Roman Catholic went into exile on his own free will! Everything was my fault!

# Narrowly Escaped Arrest by the Animal Officer!

THE BABYLONIAN EXILE WAS NOT without problems. One day I got a call.

Animal Officer of Clinton: "Sir, do you have a cat?"

ME: "Yes"

AO: "What is his color?"

ME: "Black"

AO: "What is his name?"

ME: "Roman Catholic"

AO: "Your cat has been wandering on Pratt Street. Thinking that he was a stray cat and out of compassion, somebody fed him. He ate and then he bit her. She has filed a complaint with us. Please release his medical files and know that we are coming to take him. He needs to be quarantined for 14 days!"

Roman Catholic heard this conversation. He escaped!!!!!!!!!!!!!!!!!!!!!!

The Animal Officer came with his cage, chain, lock, etc., but Roman Catholic was not there. He searched for him everywhere but did not find him.

A few days later Roman Catholic quietly returned at night and said, "I won! They lost! Where is my dinner?"

# You Should Have Air Conditioned Our Parking Lot!

On a summer day, I got into my car parked in our parking lot and went shopping. When I reached my destination and was about to get out of the car, I heard the sound: "Meow." I looked back! Guess what I saw? Roman Catholic was fast asleep on the back seat of the car! Yes, I had left the doors of the car unlocked and the windows rolled down. It was a hot day. He had jumped into my car and was sleeping there.

"Meow, what are you doing? Luckily you got into my car, but if it were another car with windows left wide open, and you had slept in it, you would have had a new address! And it is the second time you did this! Please do not do it again!"

"Oh, it's all your fault! It was a hot day and I was looking for a cool place. When I saw your car wide open, I was tempted to get in and sleep there. I yielded to the temptation and got in and made myself at home! You led me into temptation. It's all your fault!"

"Roman Catholic, no more joking with me! I am serious! Don't give me excuses."

"Dad, why don't you consider air conditioning

the whole parking lot? After all, you take a second collection during the Masses quite often. Why can't you take up a third collection to air condition the parking lot?

Aaahhh!

In this way, I—who am your son, am the security guard of the church, and am always willing to lay down my life to protect you from terrorism—might have a decent place for my job."

"Roman Catholic, you amaze me!"

# Your Garden Is of No Use!

WHEN I WENT TO CUSCO IN Peru with my groups, Fr. Robert Crasta from India was ministering in the parish. He had brought for me some seeds of Indian beans and Indian okras. They belonged to the same family of beans and okras as here but were much bigger and tastier. With much excitement I planted them in a small garden near the rectory.

Four days after planting them, I saw that the soil was completely plowed, and the seeds were on the surface! After some inquiry, I found out that it was Roman Catholic who had dug up the garden!

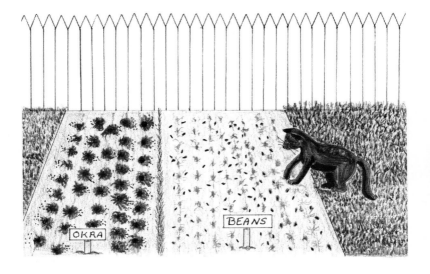

"Why did you do that?" I questioned him.

"Oh, you planted them four days ago. I did not see any bulbs and plants, so I decided to dig and find out why. They are all dead! Come and see! They will not produce any plants! Your garden is of no use!"

"Roman Catholic, please consult me before you do anything like this again! The fact is that seeds have to die before they give birth to plants! Then the plants grow and yield a rich harvest. You deprived me of my hobby!"

"As usual, you are accusing me. In reality it is the fault of Fr. Crasta and you. You planted dead seeds and blame me for it. Everything is your fault!"

# Roman Catholic: the Tour Guide

IN THE YEAR 2000, WE built a new Parish Center. As a part of the project, we bought a small piece of the neighboring property with a house on it. That house became the new rectory, and the present rectory was turned into a building for all Parish Offices. So, I invited the parish to an Open House of the new rectory.

ROMAN CATHOLIC: "Dad, the Open House is a good idea! I would like to offer a tour of our facilities. I will be the tour guide.

"I will lead them through the new rectory, show them the grounds of our newly acquired property, and bring them to the building housing all the Parish Offices. I will show them the new Parish Center with the classrooms, the new halls, and the great new kitchen. I will make them aware of the revised parking lot." (Until now cars were parked in single lanes, one behind the other like sardines in a can.) "The tour will last for twenty minutes. With a break for ten minutes in between, I can conduct three tours. No need for any tips for me; just a thank you will be enough!"

DAD: "It is a great idea! I accept your service!"

The invitation to the Open House included lunch, games, relaxation, and a tour of the church grounds by Roman Catholic. However, when the Open House began, Roman Catholic was not around.

Then I found him! "What is happening, Meow? Why are you not conducting the tours?"

"It is too hot outside. It is all your fault. You could have asked God to cut down on the heat, so that I could do the tours, but you were too lazy to pray. As a result, it is too hot, and I cannot offer the tours. It is all your fault!"

# DON'T YOU EVER FEED HIM! THAT IS AN ORDER!

ON THE DAYS OF THE Open House, I had fed Roman Catholic outside on the rectory grounds, but had forgotten to remove the plate after he had eaten. When I looked outside, I saw an opossum most busy eating the leftovers! I was glad! I sent him a silent email: "I am so happy to welcome you and give this meal! I love you!"

The following Sunday night when I went home, guess what I saw? The opossum was sitting on the steps of my rectory!

"What are you doing here?" I inquired.

"Oh, I came to the Open House," the opossum replied.

"There is no Open House today."

"Oh, when is the next one?"

"I don't remember. It is in the bulletin. Read the bulletin!" I felt very sorry for him. He was hungry. I wish I had known he was coming and would have left him a good meal!

The next Sunday I left him a big meal! I looked outside the window to see whether he was there. Guess what I saw? Two opossums were eating from my plate! I went out and said to my friend, "How come you brought another one?"

"Oh, oh, this is my neighbor. Last week you told me to read the bulletin. After reading it, I gave it to him. He likes your parish and wants to join it!!!"

"My dear opossum, I love you! You are the most intelligent opossum I have ever met!" In the silence of my heart I decided to leave a plate for him every Sunday.

However, when I entered the house, I saw an angry face! Roman Catholic said to me, "Don't you ever feed him! That is an order!" And I obeyed him! Roman Catholic was jealous!

# Getting Even with Me!

Our new Parish Center was blessed in November of 2000. The Center was a major improvement, something we needed badly! It cost us $1.5 million. Our parish was not rich at all! So the blessing of the place was a major event. Bishop Hart presided over it.

I wanted Roman Catholic to be actively involved with the dedication. And I knew that cats did not like to bathe with fresh water. However, I presumed he would understand the solemnity of the occasion, cooperate with me, and be present at the ceremony as a handsome cat. To this end, I gave him a bath with fresh water! Did he hate it! He escaped my hands, rolled up and down in the dust, and sat at the entrance to the Parish Center for the blessing.

# Father, It Was Your Cat Who Started the Fight!

St. Mary's used to have car washes during the summer from 7:30 a.m. to 11:30 a.m. One Sunday one of the volunteers said to me, "Father, there are two cats fighting on the other side of the fence. It was your cat who started it. We sprayed water on both of them to stop the argument."

One of the neighbors told me, "Father, if we leave our doors open during this heat, your cat simply moves in and sleeps on our couch!"

As previously mentioned, there were many times when I had left the doors of my car not only unlocked, but also with the windows wide open. When I would get into my driver's seat to drive away, I would often behold Roman Catholic fast asleep on the back seat.

Over and over I told him, "Don't you ever do this, Roman Catholic. Otherwise you will have a new address!" He never listened to me!

# In Your Old Age You Have Forgotten Where Chips Is

WEEKENDS AT ST. MARY'S WERE a killer for me! For years I celebrated seven Masses all alone in three different languages: five in English and one each in Spanish and Portuguese! How I did it, I don't know, but I did it. In addition, there were funerals, weddings, and baptisms in one of the languages mentioned above! After the last Mass, which was a Brazilian Mass ending at about 9:00 p.m., I was like a statue! I was numb, almost dead! I could not talk to anybody, could not see anybody, could not look at anybody! So tired I was!!! And the next morning, Monday, I had the 9:00 a.m. Mass.

I found some relief by walking to a nearby restaurant right after the last Mass. Chips Restaurant was just a five minute walk from the rectory. I sat in a corner and had a beer. Even then, I went there with paper and pen to prepare my input for the weekly bulletin!

Roman Catholic knew all of this, so every Sunday night he would wait for me near the rectory at about 9:00 p.m. He would say to me, "I know you want to go to Chips, but I also know that in your old age, you have become very forgetful. You don't know where Chips is! If you go alone, you will be lost on the way!!! But don't worry, I know where it is. I will take you there. Follow me."

He went first and I followed him. He crossed the road and waited for me to cross it, too. Then he walked on the sidewalk and I followed him. Occasionally, he stopped to see that I was really there and was not lost! As we neared our destination, he crossed the road and waited for me to cross as well. Then he said to me, "This is Chips' parking lot. The restaurant is directly in front of you. Go and enjoy yourself. I will wait for your return."

Sure enough, when I returned to the parking lot, I said loudly, "Meow, I am here!" Within seconds he was at my feet!!!

"Follow me," he said. We returned home by the same route.

Once home, I gave him a big hug, but he wanted something else. I asked, "What do you want from me?" He wanted tips!!! So I gave him some snacks. He ate them, wanted seconds, and then he bit me. That was his way of thanking me!

# Emperor of 282 Airline Road

I retired from St. Mary's on May 30, 2012. Roman Catholic and I moved into our new home—a mobile home in Westbrook. He did not like it, and neither did I, but we had to accept the reality.

Then came a call from the manager of my mobile home: "Your cat cannot be an outdoor cat. You have three weeks to comply with our order, or else we will come and take him!" The message: the electric chair was ready for him for a crime he did not commit!

Panicked, I began to look for a new place, but there was none! Out of despair I called Judy Schiffer, one of our parishioners and a friend of mine. Judy was a Eucharistic minister and an advisor to me on programs for adult education and spirituality. She invited me to come and see the apartment she and her husband Bob had next to their house. I loved the apartment! Roman Catholic and I moved in!

Roman Catholic inspected the property! The next day he wandered around and entered the house of Judy and Bob and quickly exited. The third day he inspected everything again including Judy and Bob's house, and he gave *summa cum laude* to everything! He fell in love with their property but went a step further. He declared ownership of their house, their grounds, and their swimming pool! He became the owner and they his tenants! He would give them commands and they had to obey him!

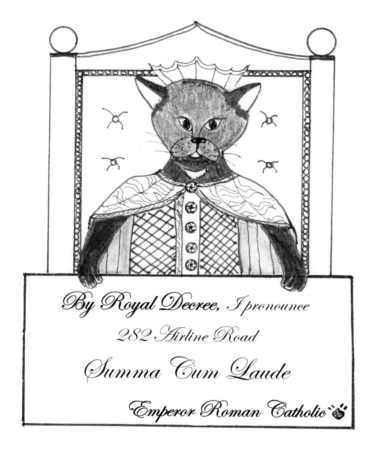

*By Royal Decree, I pronounce*

*282 Airline Road*

*Summa Cum Laude*

*Emperor Roman Catholic*

If Bob disagreed with him on anything, they would have a big argument and Roman Catholic would go and bite him. In the end the one who won always was Roman Catholic!

On that day Roman Catholic became Roman Catholic!!! He experienced a complete transformation, a new life, and a new beginning. He realized that there is always Easter Sunday after Good Friday!

On August 29, 2012 when Roman Catholic met Judy and Bob, he hit the gold mine again. On that day he was crowned the Emperor of 282 Airline Road in Clinton, Connecticut in the United States of America!!!

Every morning, the Emperor would go to their house at six o'clock and ask for the menu. He ordered his breakfast. Then he slept on Judy's lap. Later he slept on a stool covered with a nice towel. He had his lunch with them and had dinner there too! At about eight o'clock at night, he would say to Judy, "Now take me to my Dad." He slept in my apartment!

# ROMAN CATHOLIC DID NOT BELIEVE IN HEAVEN!

AS AN OUTSTANDING CATHOLIC, Roman Catholic always recited his night prayers before retiring. However, after being crowned as the Emperor of 282 Airline Road in Clinton, I saw a change. When the night prayers he was reciting said, "I believe in heaven," he left it out! He would not say, "I believe in heaven."

I asked him why he left it out. He reasoned that life at 282 Airline Road was so good, that he could not believe that there was going to be anything better than that!!! This was heaven on earth for him! And I

respected his approach! After all, God understands our sincere and profound convictions. God is a God of love and not a God of rules and orders.

We love you, Roman Catholic!

# Security Guard at the Vineyard

Soon after settling down at our new home, Roman Catholic volunteered for a summer job as a security guard at Chamard Vineyard next door. He took on the duties of protecting the plants from animals wanting to eat them and the grapes from thieves wanting to steal them. He did a great job with his duties.

There were concerns, however. Did he go to the bar there and come home full of spirit?

# The Sun Rises. The Sun Sets.

KING SAUL, THE FIRST KING of the Israelites, King David, and King Solomon experienced sunrise and sunset in their lives. Roman Catholic was no exception. He had shown me some weaknesses at times, but indirectly.

I was away for a week at the end of November 2015. My friend Maryanne looked after him twice daily. He was great as usual! However, upon my return on December 5, 2015, the sunset became obvious. He was waiting for my return. We took him to his doc. He advised us to grant him eternal rest. He had some growth in his stomach.

Judy held him in her arms and said, "When I come there, I will see you." He bowed his head as if to say, "Yes." He laid down on the doctor's table and breathed his last. We wept!

One of the main reasons for his long life of nineteen years was a gift that Judy and Bob gave him about four years ago. They sponsored the cleaning of his teeth.

He lost ten teeth, but he was eating better and was healthier than before.

We brought him home and laid him to rest on our grounds. Maryanne put flowers on the site. Later she put a plant there and it is growing.

Eternal rest grant unto him, O Lord. Amen.

We love you, Roman Catholic! We love you very much, Meow! You were God sent to me and to Judy and Bob! We feel you are with us at all times. We imagine we are holding you in our hands and petting you! We say good-bye until we meet. We love you!

# "The Lord Hears the Cry of the Poor!" "It Is True," says Francis

ON MEMORIAL DAY WEEKEND OF the year 2016, we began to hear repeated cries of a cat. It was not meowing, rather a cat crying desperately. We heard it for three days. Not knowing where it came from, we ignored it, hoping it was only temporary. It only grew worse.

Judy went searching for the cat but did not find it. Meanwhile the cries of the cat were becoming louder and more desperate. Judy leaned against the wall of my apartment and said, "There is suffering in the world."

I said, "Amen."

After one week's search, Judy located it! A cat was sitting near the top of a tall tree by our house. Most probably it was hiding from animals chasing it. It was there for about two weeks and was hungry, thirsty, frightened by thunder, lightning, darkness, and rain.

We tried to make him come down, but he did not. We used a long stick to bring him down, but he climbed higher. The Clinton Fire Department was most willing to help but could not bring its truck near the tree. We were without hope.

Suddenly, Forgotten Felines in Westbrook called
me and gave me the name of a professional tree
climber. He came, climbed the tree, caught the cat,
and gave him to us! We rescued him!! A miracle!!! We
named him "Francis."

I kept him, fed him, and looked after him. He
did well in the first week, but then he became ill. He
had an infection. The doctor performed surgery and
hospitalized him. When he came home, he did well.

However, a week later he was sick again. We took him to the doctor three times! He had three surgeries and hospitalizations. He had become very skinny. His skeleton was showing. There was temptation to give up, but Judy and I would not allow it.

Miraculously, after the third surgery Francis regained his health, began to eat well, and put on weight. Now he has become a big and beautiful cat. He is happy! Every day he goes out, enters Judy and Bob's house, eats with them and sleeps there! He always sleeps upside down! Francis has become a delightful cat! He thinks he is the king of the world!

Francis hit a gold mine! A miracle took place!!!

# "Fr. Michael, Tonight I Must Eat in Your House," said Zach

NEAR THE FRONT DOOR OF my apartment, there was, and still is, a little hole in the ground. Plates with Roman Catholic's food and water were next to it.

Suddenly, I saw a mouse rushing out of the hole, grabbing some dry food from the plate with his little mouth, and rushing back to the hole. I noticed that once he succeeded in his first expedition, he came back again within a few seconds. Of course, he maintained his high speed lest he be caught by the immigration officer, Roman Catholic, when he was still with us! Again he succeeded in his adventure! He was in and out at least seventeen times! He was hungry!

The next time he came, Roman Catholic saw him!!! I had thought that the mouse would be sent to the electric chair right away! But no—Roman Catholic did nothing! He had allowed the mouse to eat his food. Later, when Francis appeared on the scene, he too welcomed the mouse to his table! A miracle!

Judy and I named the mouse "Zach," because he was small. St. Luke's Gospel tells us that when Jesus was passing through the city of Jericho, He met a tax collector by the name of Zacchaeus. Because Zacchaeus was short in stature, he climbed a tree to see Jesus. Jesus said to him, "Zacchaeus, come down! Today I must stay in your house!"

In an analogous way, Zach said to me, "Fr. Michael, today I must eat in your house!"

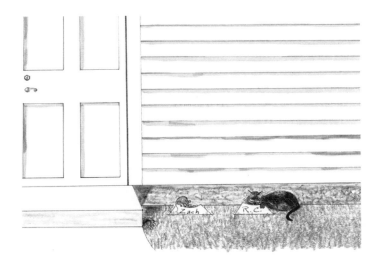

I told this story to my niece Jyothi in California. She said that I should deny him a visa and stop his entry. Why? Because he and his family would take possession of my apartment, and it would not be healthy for me.

I said to her, "He cannot have a family, because he is single and not married!

"Uncle, soon he will meet his bride and will start a family."

"Then I will marry them and help the newly married couple to live happily ever after!"

Let us say together: "Amen! Let us plan on going to the wedding!"

# I Am the Greatest!

When I was small, there was no money! We were poor. If we had some rice to fill up our bellies, we were lucky! I was longing for a pet but got none.

Just then, my parents got a pair of water buffaloes to plough the rice fields. Since I was the chairperson of the welcoming committee, I went to meet them. One of them—who was young, energetic, and handsome—was kneeling on the ground and digging. I looked at him and he looked at me. We made eye contact.

"What are you doing, you silly buffalo?" I asked.

"I am turning the world upside down. Get ready to walk on your head!" he said. I loved his answer. So I made him my pet and gave him a beautiful name: "Pakdu". That was a name I had remembered from a high school play. And since he ploughed the land so well, I gave him an honorary doctorate in agriculture from my own university. So he became Dr. Pakdu. His last name being the same as mine.

Most importantly, I wanted him to be a Catholic. So with the hope of baptizing him, I taught him the Baltimore Catechism. Do you remember it? It consisted of questions and answers. If you memorized them and answered the questions correctly, you were a good Catholic.

"Dr. Pakdu, who created you?" I quizzed him.

"God," he said.

"Why did God create you?"

"To love Him, to serve Him, and to enjoy eternal bliss with Him."

After the long and boring catechism classes, we would relax and rest. And he would say to me, "I am the greatest!"

"Why do you say that?"

"Because God created me as the greatest," he responded.

"But earlier you said that God created you to love Him and to serve Him."

"Oh, that was because I wanted to get a snack from you. The only way I can get anything out of you is by giving you an answer you want to hear. Now that I got my snack, I am free to tell you the truth: I am the greatest. I can defeat anyone!"

"Dr. Pakdu, you are my pet. I love you and will always love you, but I refuse to baptize you. You are too worldly, your ego is big, and you are not converted to qualify for baptism."

Dr. Pakdu was never baptized, but to this day I remember him and love him. I believe he is with God enjoying eternal bliss with Him!

# Do You Practice What You Preach?

ON A SUMMER DAY TWO years ago, I had the 8:00 a.m. Mass at St. Frances Cabrini Church in North Haven. I had arrived early, so I was sitting outside the church on a beautiful morning. A young squirrel would come very close to me and then run away. It was a daily routine for three days. On the fourth day he took courage and said, "what are you doing here? You should be inside the church!"

"I am preparing my homily."

"So, you are a preacher. Tell me, do you practice what you preach?"

"What? You should not be asking me such a question. You have crossed the line!"

"I am sorry! It is my way of saying that I am hungry and of asking you for something to eat."

"Oh my dear baby squirrel, I love you! I don't have anything now, but tomorrow I will give you a banquet."

When tomorrow came, he approached me. "Did you bring it?"

"Yes, here it is," I said. "May I serve it?"

"Yes, please do so. I am going home to bring my family here. We eat together as a family."

After the Mass I noticed that they had not only eaten the meal but also had cleaned their plates! Then I realized that my friend, the young squirrel, came from a good family!

Since the family was so respectful, I thought that they should be baptized and made Catholics. I approached the baby squirrel and said, "I invite all of you to join my church. I will put you in the religious formation program which prepares people for baptism. At the Easter Vigil I will baptize you with triple immersion! It is a good thing for you!"

"Oh, no! We are in the process of starting our own church. It will be for all animals—both wild and tame. My parents will be pastors, and I will take up the collection. I invite you to our services and to give us a word of encouragement!"

"Oh baby squirrel, I love you!
Good luck
to you!
I love
all of you!"

# Pet Owners, Animal Owners, Fishermen, Butchers, Hunters, Everyone

ALL FARMERS, ALL THOSE WHO own animals, and all those who come into contact with animals:

~ *Treat them well with love.*

~ *Give them the best treatment and the best food.*

~ *Farmers: it is they who earn you your daily bread!*

~ *Pet owners: it is they who bring joy to you.*

~ *Those who come into contact with animals: realize that they are looking for food, love, and acceptance from you. Treat them well!*

~ *Fishermen and those who fish as a hobby: your catch is within your power! Treat them as humanely as you can without causing them more pain or suffering.*

~ *Butchers and hunters: treat your animals humanely—with minimum pain, suffering, and torture.*

You should not hurt innocent animals deliberately and cruelly. They can't defend their rights. That, however, does not give you license to abuse them. They will cry out to the Lord, and the Lord hears the cry of the poor.

All animals are God's creation and are God's gift to us! Love them and treat them with good food, good shelter, and lots of love. They are in your hands and at your disposal. You can abuse them or treat them with love. Treat them with love please.

AMEN.

# AFTERWORD

*Roman Catholic sleeps, and while he does he
dreams some dreams of people he met long ago...*

*Fr. Michael, who took him in for "just one night"
and then another & another, 'til he had a new home.*

*Together they had many adventures, all of which
became special treasures. While Roman Catholic
was not exactly angelic, he taught Fr. Michael
many important things, like the importance of the
virtues of patience and understanding, and above
all, gentleness with animals. Fr. Michael taught
Roman Catholic about what love really is, even
when he did not think the cat's action was loving.*

*The first hint of Roman Catholic's "conversion"
was when he brought Fr. Michael a birthday
present, because Fr. Michael did not know that
cats actually know how to love their owners.
Roman Catholic loved Fr. Michael very much,
but not having hands like humans, nor a human
voice, he would gently "bite" Fr. Michael as a
sign of affection.*

*Over the many years they were together,
Fr. Michael and Roman Catholic learned much
from each other. So, as you were reading these
stories, we hope you found them not just amusing,
but also warm and tender, about a feline friend
and how both of them learned to care for each
other through the years.*

*~ Dianne Coyle*

# Roman Cat🐾holic
## (1997-2015)

# An Outstanding Cat